HOW TO SCARE A GHOST

by Jean Reagan

illustrated by Lee Wildish

ALFRED A. KNOPF NEW YORK

For Jane, who always "rocks" Halloween
—J.R.

THIS IS A BORZOI BOOK PUBLISHED BY ALFRED A. KNOPF

Text copyright © 2018 by Jean Reagan
Jacket art and interior illustrations copyright © 2018 by Lee Wildish

Visit us on the Web! rhcbooks.com

Educators and librarians, for a variety of teaching tools, visit us at RHTeachersLibrarians.com

Library of Congress Cataloging-in-Publication Data
Names: Reagan, Jean, author. | Wildish, Lee, illustrator. Title: How to scare a ghost / by Jean Reagan ;
Illustrated by Lee Wildish. Description: First edition. | New York : Alfred A. Knopf, [2018] |
Summary: Halloween is the best time to catch, entertain, and make friends with a ghost.
Identifiers: LCCN 2017044039 (print) | LCCN 2017056384 (ebook) | ISBN 978-1-5247-0190-1 (trade) |
ISBN 978-1-5247-0191-8 (lib. bdg.) | ISBN 978-1-5247-0192-5 (ebook)
Subjects: | CYAC: Halloween—Fiction. | Ghosts—Fiction.
Classification: LCC PZ7.R2354 (ebook) | LCC PZ7.R2354 Hgt 2018 (print) |
DDC [E]—dc23

The text of this book is set in 18-point Goudy Old Style.
The illustrations were created digitally.

MANUFACTURED IN CHINA
August 2018
10 9 8 7 6 5 4 3 2 1
First Edition

Do you want to scare a ghost? The easiest,
spookiest time to try is . . . Halloween!

First, you have to find one.

HOW TO ATTRACT A GHOST:

* Hide scarecrows
in your yard.

No ghost yet? Keep your eyes wide open while you do more Halloweeny things—even at school.

GHOSTS CAN'T RESIST:

* Bobbing for apples.

On whiteboard:
$1 + 1 = 2$ $2 - 1 = 1$
$2 + 2 = 4$ $3 - 2 = 1$

HAPPY HALLOWEEN

* Cupcakes.

* Games.

* Glitter.

Still no luck? Don't give up. Try one last trick—MAKE **SCAAAAAAARY** SOUNDS:

✳ A witch's   "Heeee

          heeee

heeee!"

* An owl's

"HOOO! HOOO!

Hooo! Hooo!"

* And an eerie, ghostly

"BOOOOOOOOO!"

Yes! You found one! But is the ghost *real* . . .
or just a kid in a costume?

HOW TO TELL IF A GHOST IS REAL:

✱ Instead of walking, ghosts float.

✱ They never, ever open doors.

✱ Ghosts are only visible to kids and cats.
 Not to grown-ups. Not to dogs.

Okay—your ghost is real. Time to get **SCARY**...!

* Pop out with your most
frightening face.

* Make a gigantic
monster shadow.

* Read spooky, creepy stories.

Your ghost might say, "Ghosts
aren't scared of *anything*!"

". . . except . . ."

VROOOOOOOOOM!

BOO!-Time
Stories

VROOOOOOOOM!

Uh-oh! *Too* scary. Help your ghost calm down with a cup of warm cider.

Promise "No more scaring!" and instead . . .

Play together!

HOW TO PLAY WITH A GHOST:

* Take turns riding
   piggyback. Wheeeeee!

* Put on a magic show.

* Scare other people,
just a teeny bit.

WHAT *NOT* TO PLAY WITH A GHOST:

* Seesaw. (When a ghost plops
down, it doesn't even budge.)

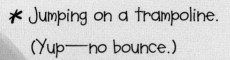

* Jumping on a trampoline.
(Yup—no bounce.)

* Hide-and-seek. (Ghosts
are *too* good at hiding.)

It's almost time to trick-or-treat. . . . Your ghost probably wants a costume, too!

HOW TO CHOOSE A COSTUME:

✱ Be your favorite thing: A soccer ball.
A sparkly red robot. A banana split.

✱ Be something scary: A skeleton.
A witch. A vacuum cleaner.

* Team up together and be: A traffic light.

Remember, a ghost in a costume can be seen by
everyone. But don't worry—your parents will just think
you made a new friend!

Ghosts know *nothing* about trick-or-treating,
so share your tips.

HOW TO TRICK-OR-TREAT:

★ Don't go through doors. Knock and yell,
"Trick-or-treat!"

✱ Then say, as fast as you can,

THANK-YOU-VERY-MUCH-GOOD-BYE!

and *zoooooooom* to the next house.

✱ Remind your ghost not to float too high.

AAGH! No feet!

Now wish everyone . . .